A MAMMOTH MISTAKE

Judy Waite
Illustrated by Sarah Warburton

Rigby

It all begin when Dad saw the advertisement in the paper:

CHILDREN'S ARCHAEOLOGICAL DIG

PLACES STILL AVAILABLE.
WORK WITH A HIGHLY
QUALIFIED ARCHAEOLOGIST.
YOU COULD DISCOVER
THE TREASURES OF
AN ANCIENT WORLD.

**CALL PROFESSOR NORMAN
AT: 555-7867**

AFTER ALL, YOU NEVER KNOW ...

"This looks good, Rachel," said Dad. "It'll give you something to do over vacation."

"What's wrong with watching television?" I asked.

Dad frowned. "You need to be out in the fresh air," he said.

"But I don't like arky-whatsit-things. They're boring," I said.

"You liked that museum I took you to last summer," Dad said.

I didn't answer. The truth was, I had NOT liked the museum. The only good thing had been the gift shop. I'd bought Monty there.

Monty was a little carved woolly mammoth made about fourteen thousand years ago.

Well, he wasn't really that old. He was just a copy of a tool ancient people had used. The real one was in the museum inside a glass case. I kept him in his plastic display box.

I gave Dad a "take pity on me" look. It didn't work.

At ten o'clock the next morning, I was on an archaeological dig. I took Monty with me.

Right from the start, I didn't get along with Professor Norman. He had bought this site, a crumbling old house with a huge overgrown yard, because it was of great archaeological interest.

"It is surprising how much we can learn from old things, even something like ancient garbage," Professor Norman told us, soon after we arrived.

All of the other children looked very interested. They looked as if they wouldn't mind at all being up to their elbows in ancient garbage.

But I couldn't help it. My thoughts just sort of jumped out of my mouth.

"Yuck!" I said. "You won't get me digging around in that!"

Professor Norman glared at me. After that he began to pick on me. He gave me the dirtiest, most boring jobs to do.

By lunchtime, I was really fed up. I sat on my own, munching my sandwiches. The only company I had was Monty. I'd brought him so I could ask Professor Norman questions about him. Except that, after Professor Norman had been so horrible, I didn't feel like asking him anything.

I took Monty out of his display box. The label on the box said that he was really a tool that ancient people used for hunting. Perhaps he could hunt out some ancient treasure for me now.

"Time to get back to work!" said Professor Norman. "Get the wheelbarrow. We've got piles of mud to move."

"Oh no . . ." I began, but Professor Norman glared at me again, and I changed my mind. I quickly slipped Monty into my pocket. Then I went to get the wheelbarrow.

That's when the real trouble began.

"I've found some sort of ornament!"
shouted one of the children. He was holding
something small and muddy. I knew right
away what it was. Monty had fallen out of
my pocket into the mud.

Still, it shouldn't have been a problem. Professor Norman would know that Monty was only a copy. I walked forward, about to ask for him back.

"Stand back," growled Professor Norman. "This could be the find of the century."

Professor Norman lifted Monty with
a pair of tweezers.

He carried Monty to the table that was set
up for "finds" at the side of the yard. He stared
at Monty through a magnifying glass.

I was feeling sick. Any minute now
Professor Norman would realize he'd been
tricked and come roaring back.

But that didn't happen. Professor Norman
hurried over with his mobile phone in his hand.

"I've called the television news," he said,
"and they'll be here soon."

I tried to tell him then, I really did. "Professor Norman, I . . ."

"Hurry up and get back to work," Professor Norman said to me. "This is my big chance. I want this to look like a busy site, where everyone is happy."

"But I just . . ."

At that moment a man and woman appeared. The man was carrying a TV camera. Professor Norman rubbed his hands together.

"Welcome," he said. "I'm sure your viewers will want to know about this story . . ."

I couldn't stand it any longer. Apart from anything else, I wanted Monty back.

"Actually," I said loudly, "he's mine."

Professor Norman looked at me as if he wished I were about fourteen thousand years away. The TV people smiled kindly, but they kept on setting up the camera.

"I can prove it." I showed them the plastic box, and pointed to the label.

Wesley Hill Museum
Copy of an ancient hunting tool carved
from reindeer antler.

The TV people suddenly seemed very interested. "So, Professor Norman—didn't you know it was fake?" asked the TV woman.

"I . . ." Professor Norman started backing away toward the house. "Umm . . . of course I did! It was just a joke," he said, but his face was bright red. He definitely wasn't laughing.

"But you told us when you called that you'd found an ancient tool," said the cameraman.

"I . . ." Professor Norman began to mutter and mumble. "Anyone can make a mistake, can't they?"

The TV people didn't look pleased. They'd
been dragged all this way just for Monty.
Professor Norman looked even less pleased.

"I want my mammoth back," I said.

Professor Norman glared at me. He threw
Monty on the ground, then he ran up the
yard and into the house.

And that put an end to our day. The TV people were still there when I left. I guess they wanted to talk to Professor Norman again. It wouldn't be the kind of news story he'd wanted.

Dad said that perhaps I would have had more fun watching TV after all. The funny thing was, I didn't want to. Instead, I went out into the warm summer evening with Monty and a wheelbarrow and began digging.

After all, you never know . . .